A NOTE TO PARENTS

Reading Aloud with Your Child

Research shows that reading books aloud is the single most valuable support parents can provide in helping children learn to read.

- Be a ham! The more enthusiasm you display, the more your child will enjoy the book.
- Run your finger underneath the words as you read to signal that the print carries the story.
- Leave time for examining the illustrations more closely; encourage your child to find things in the pictures.
- Invite your youngster to join in whenever there's a repeated phrase in the text.
- Link up events in the book with similar events in your child's life.
- If your child asks a question, stop and answer it. The book can be a means to learning more about your child's thoughts.

Listening to Your Child Read Aloud

The support of your attention and praise is absolutely crucial to your child's continuing efforts to learn to read.

- If your child is learning to read and asks for a word, give it immediately so that the meaning of the story is not interrupted. DO NOT ask your child to sound out the word.
- On the other hand, if your child initiates the act of sounding out, don't intervene.
- If your child is reading along and makes what is called a miscue, listen for the sense of the miscue. If the word "road" is substituted for the word "street," for instance, no meaning is lost. Don't stop the reading for a correction.
- If the miscue makes no sense (for example, "horse" for "house"), ask your child to reread the sentence because you're not sure you understand what's just been read.
- Above all else, enjoy your child's growing command of print and make sure you give lots of praise. *You are your child's first teacher — and the most important one. Praise from you is critical for further risk-taking and learning.*

— Priscilla Lynch
Ph.D., New York University
Educational Consultant

To William Kubetin
— K.M.

To Ross
— M.S.

Text copyright © 1997 by Kate McMullan.
Illustrations copyright © 1997 by Mavis Smith.
All rights reserved. Published by Scholastic Inc.
HELLO READER! and CARTWHEEL BOOKS and associated logos
are trademarks and/or registered trademarks of Scholastic Inc.

Library of Congress Cataloging-in-Publication Data
McMullan, Kate.
    Fluffy's Thanksgiving/by Kate McMullan; illustrated by Mavis Smith.
        p.   cm. — (Hello reader! Level 3)
    "Cartwheel books."
    Summary: After starring as an ear of corn in his school's Thanksgiving play, the classroom guinea pig enjoys his holiday at Maxwell's home, where he scares Grammy and battles a monster.
    ISBN 0-590-37215-7
    [1. Guinea pigs — Fiction.   2. Thanksgiving — Fiction.   3. Schools — Fiction.]
    I. Smith, Mavis, ill.   II. Title.   III. Series.
PZ7.M2295Fj   1997
[E] — dc21
                                                            97-17948
                                                                CIP
                                                                 AC

10   9   8   7   6   5   4   3   8   9/9   0/0   01   02

Printed in the U.S.A.   24
First printing, November 1997

FLUFFY'S

THANKSGIVING

by Kate McMullan

Illustrated by Mavis Smith

Hello Reader! — Level 3

SCHOLASTIC INC.

New York   Toronto   London   Auckland   Sydney

Fluffy Takes a Bow

"You are all going to be in a Thanksgiving play," Ms. Day told her class.

"Even Fluffy?" asked Maxwell.

"I think we can find a small part for Fluffy," said Ms. Day.

A small part? thought Fluffy.

I want a big part.

"Who would like to be the chief?"
asked Ms. Day.
I'm your chief! thought Fluffy.
"How about Maxwell?" said Ms. Day
"Yes," said Maxwell.
"Who wants to be Squanto?" asked Ms. Day.
Me, me, me! thought Fluffy.
"Wade will be Squanto," said Ms. Day.

"Raise your hand if you would like
to play a Pilgrim," said Ms. Day.
Hello! I'm raising my paw!
thought Fluffy.
But Ms. Day didn't see Fluffy's paw.
She picked Emma and six other
kids to play Pilgrims.

"And who wants to play the turkey?"
asked Ms. Day.
It's not my first choice,
thought Fluffy.
But, hey — gobble, gobble!
"I'll do it," called Jasmine.

"Ms. Day?" said Maxwell.
"What part do we have for Fluffy?"
**Yeah! What part do we have
for Fluffy?** thought Fluffy.
"Fluffy would make a cute pumpkin,"
said Jasmine.

I don't think so, thought Fluffy.

"Fluffy's too fat to be a zucchini," said Wade.

Who asked you? thought Fluffy.

"Ms. Day!" called Emma.

"I know the perfect part for Fluffy!" She whispered her idea to Ms. Day. Fluffy didn't hear what she said.

The whole school came to see
the Thanksgiving play.
The curtain went up.
"Thank you, Squanto,"
said Emma the Pilgrim,
"for your gift of corn."

Emma the Pilgrim held up
an ear of corn.
The ear of corn was Fluffy.
Then Emma put the ear of corn
into her pocket, and the play
went on.

The ear of corn stuck its head
out of the pocket.
It sniffed at the feast table.
The audience started to giggle.
Emma the Pilgrim walked
very close to the feast table.
The ear of corn forgot all about
being an ear of corn.
It climbed out of the pocket
and onto the table.

It ran over to a pile
of onions and yams and pumpkins
and other ears of corn.

The audience laughed.
But the ear of corn didn't notice.
It was too busy gobbling its own
Thanksgiving feast.

When the play was over,

Ms. Day's class took a bow.

The audience clapped and clapped.

Emma the Pilgrim held up the ear of corn.

The audience cheered!

The ear of corn gazed out at everyone

clapping and cheering.

Yes! thought the ear of corn.

Today a star is born!

Fluffy's Great Escape

Fluffy went home with Maxwell
for Thanksgiving break.
Maxwell showed Fluffy
to his little sister, Violet.
"Ohhh, sweet little piggy!" said Violet.
Yuck! thought Fluffy.

Maxwell showed Fluffy to his dad.

"What do you call that thing?" asked his dad.

Guinea pig, thought Fluffy.

But you can call me SIR.

On Thanksgiving morning,
Maxwell helped his mom
wash the celery.
Fluffy nibbled the celery leaves.
The doorbell rang.
"It's Grammy!" said Maxwell's mom.
"Maxwell, quick! Put the guinea pig
back in his cage!"

Maxwell's mom and dad ran to the door
to greet Grammy.
Maxwell hurried Fluffy back to
his cage in the den.
Then he went to meet Grammy, too.

But the gate of Fluffy's cage
was not closed all the way.
Fluffy pushed it with his nose
until the opening was as wide as he was.
Then he jumped out of his cage.
Celery leaves, thought Fluffy,
here I come!

"Let me take your suitcase
to the guest room, Grammy,"
said Maxwell's dad.
"I can carry it," said Grammy.
"Let me help you,"
said Maxwell's mom.
"I can do it," said Grammy.
"I'm not *that* old."

Grammy walked down the hall
to the guest room.
Fluffy walked up the hall to the kitchen.
He was sniffing the air
when he heard a scream.
"Oh!" someone cried. "A rat!"
A rat? thought Fluffy. **How awful!**
Fluffy turned around
and ran back the other way.

Grammy hurried into the bathroom
and shut the door.
Maxwell's mom ran down the hall.
"Where are you, Grammy?" she called.
Fluffy ran into the guest room and
hid behind a wastebasket.
If there is one thing I don't like,
he thought, **it's a rat.**

Maxwell's dad knocked on
the bathroom door.
"Are you all right, Grammy?" he called.
"I saw a rat!" Grammy called back.
"A rat?" cried Maxwell's dad.
"IIow awful!"
Grammy opened the door a crack.
"If there is one thing I don't like,"
she said, "it's a rat."

Maxwell and his mom and dad walked
Grammy to the guest room.
"Don't worry, Grammy," said Maxwell's mom.
"There are no rats in this house."
"Yes, there are!" Grammy cried.
"I see one now!"

"That's not a rat, Grammy," said Maxwell.

"That's a guinea pig."

"A guinea pig!" said Grammy.

"Why, I love guinea pigs!"

Maxwell showed Fluffy to Grammy.

"My!" said Grammy.

"What a fine big handsome fellow you are!"

Grammy, thought Fluffy.

You are one smart woman!

Fluffy's Horrible Monster

"No, Maxwell," said his mom.

"The guinea pig cannot sleep in your room."

"Please!" said Maxwell.

"It's Fluffy's last night here."

His mom shook her head.

"May I say 'Good night' to Fluffy?"
Maxwell asked. "Please?"
"Okay," said his mom.
Maxwell picked up Teddy
and ran into the den.

"Good night, Fluffy," said Maxwell.
Fluffy was already asleep.
"I'm sorry that you can't sleep with me,"
said Maxwell.
"But Teddy can sleep with you
so you won't be scared.
Sweet dreams!"

Maxwell put the bear in Fluffy's cage.
Fluffy did not wake up.
He was dreaming that he was chasing
a guinea pig named Duke.

In the middle of the night,
Fluffy woke up feeling hungry.
His black eyes searched his cage.
And there in the moonlight he saw it.
Over by his food bowl —
a horrible monster.

It was a giant!

It had a long snout and small, beady eyes.

It looked mean — very, very mean.

Get out of my cage, Fluffy growled,

and I mean now!

Fluffy thought he saw

the monster show his fangs.

I'm not kidding! Fluffy growled.

Fluffy thought he heard the monster

growl back.

**I want you out by the time
I count to three,** said Fluffy.
One!
Two!
Three!
The monster didn't move.

**Maybe the monster doesn't go
to school,** Fluffy thought.
**Maybe the monster doesn't
know about counting.**

Okay, you asked for it, monster,
thought Fluffy. **Here I come!**
Fluffy charged.

The two rolled around the cage.
Fluffy growled and hissed.
He bit and kicked.
He clawed and scratched.
It was a terrible battle!

When it was all over,
Fluffy's left ear flopped over.
His right eye was half-closed.
His fur was a mess.

But the monster lay face down
on the floor of Fluffy's cage.
**You should have run when
you had the chance,**
growled Fluffy.

On Monday,
Maxwell took Fluffy back to school.
He made a report to the class.
"It was fun to have Fluffy
stay at my house," Maxwell said.

"When he goes to your house, remember—Fluffy likes to sleep with a teddy bear."